Toby, the Almost Forgotten Toboggan

A merry little Christmas story

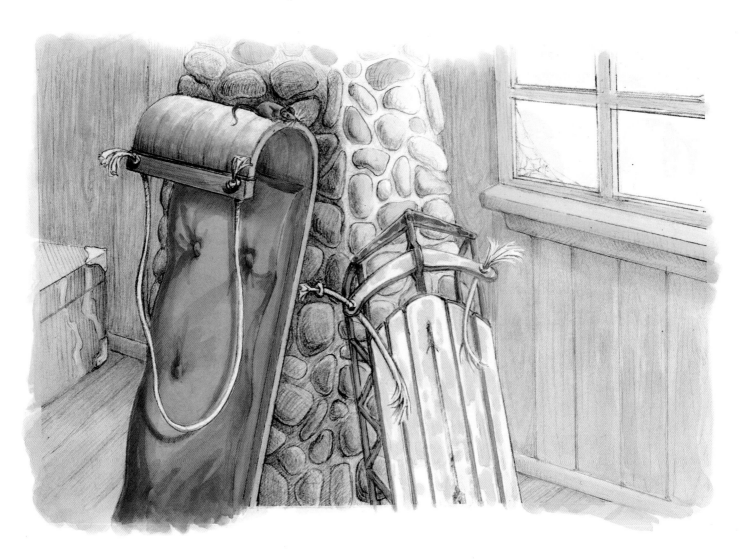

by Karen Votraw-Gysen
illustrated by Chris Bond Sullivan

AuthorHouse™
1663 Liberty Drive
Bloomington, IN 47403
www.authorhouse.com
Phone: 1 (800) 839-8640

This book is printed on acid-free paper.

ISBN: 978-1-7283-3524-7 (sc)
ISBN: 978-1-7283-3526-1 (hc)
ISBN: 978-1-7283-3525-4 (e)

Library of Congress Control Number: 2020903390

Printed in the United States of America

Published by AuthorHouse 07/14/2020

authorHOUSE®

*In memory of my twin brother, Kent,
a gentle and caring man.*

*For grandparents everywhere who love to share
the past with their grandchildren. What joy!*

Chapter 1

"Ahhhhh, hummm. Ahhhhhhhh, hummmmmm. Ahhhhhhhhhhhhh," were heard in the attic of an old farmhouse in far northern Vermont.

"Stop that sighing! I'm tired of hearing it," said a little voice coming from the other side of the chimney.

"Who's, who is that?" asked the sighing, shaky voice.

"It's Sally, Sally the sled. You can't see me. I'm leaning up against the other side of the chimney."

"Sally the sled? You mean you ended up here in the attic too? This is Toby, Toby the toboggan."

"Yes, I know who you are. We used to be in the old barn when the family lived here. I've heard your cries and sighing for years now. And I just can't take it anymore!"

"Well, I'm sad. Especially at this time of the year, watching the snow coming down outside. I can just barely see it out the little window on the other side of the attic. This was when the kids would bring us out to the big hill and ride us for hours. Oh, how I miss the brisk, cold, snowy days. And all the fun! But I'm totally covered with dust now. My wood slats are splintery, and my leather seat pad is almost dried out. I guess we've been forgotten," said Toby.

Sally sighed. "Oh, I miss it too. The kids, their friends, and parents all having a great time sledding and sliding, laughing and squealing as they raced down the hill. At least we weren't thrown in the trash. Or worse yet, used as firewood."

"Shhhhh," said Toby. "I think I hear someone opening the front door. Shhhh."

An energetic gray-haired lady opened the front door. "Oh, it's good to get out of the cold! Even better to be in the home where I was raised. And back in the little town where we both grew up."

"You're right, Granny. It's great to be spending this holiday in the old house where I picked you up for our first date. Your father sternly reminded me about the 10:00 p.m. curfew. I sure was scared. Wouldn't have brought you home one minute late," said the spry old man with a shock of white hair falling on his brow.

"Well, Grandpa, we've come a long way since those days. Married forty-five years, two children, and now two darling grandchildren who will be flying in from California tomorrow to spend an old-fashioned Christmas with us. I'm so excited to share what we experienced way back then."

"Right you are, my sweetie. We'd better get this place tidied up, warm, and ready for a very smart eight-year-old boy and a pretty, little six-year-old princess." said Grandpa. So they brought in the groceries from their car, made the beds in the upstairs bedrooms, and stacked wood and started fires in the cookstove and fireplace to get the chill off the 150-year-old farmhouse.

Chapter 2

"Jimmy? Julie? Are you dressed and ready?" Mom called out from the kitchen of their modern home in the Bay area of California the next morning. "It's almost time to drive to the airport. It's a long flight from California to Vermont."

"Dad, can I bring the skateboard I got from Santa?" asked Jimmy.

"Mommy, I want to bring the Barbie Dream House Santa gave me," said Julie.

"No," answered Dad. "You can't pack such large gifts. You'll be back in a week to play with your new presents."

"I'm not leaving without my iPad," shouted Jimmy.

"Me neither," added Julie.

"That's fine," said Dad. "You can easily carry those in your backpacks."

Jimmy and Julie came stomping downstairs, disappointed they couldn't pack all their new treasures. But they were equally excited to be going on a big airplane and fly across the United States to visit their grandparents for Christmas vacation. Jimmy and Julie had never been to Vermont. They had heard stories about the village where Granny and Grandpa had grown up, about snow-covered forests and cold frosty nights with a roaring fireplace. They wanted to see it all. This was going to be their very first adventure without Mom and Dad. They were excited but maybe a bit frightened.

"Hurry up, kids. We need to get you to the airport. We want to meet the attendant who will be with you during the long flight," said Mom. The luggage and backpacks were loaded into the family van, and off to the airport they went very early the morning after Christmas.

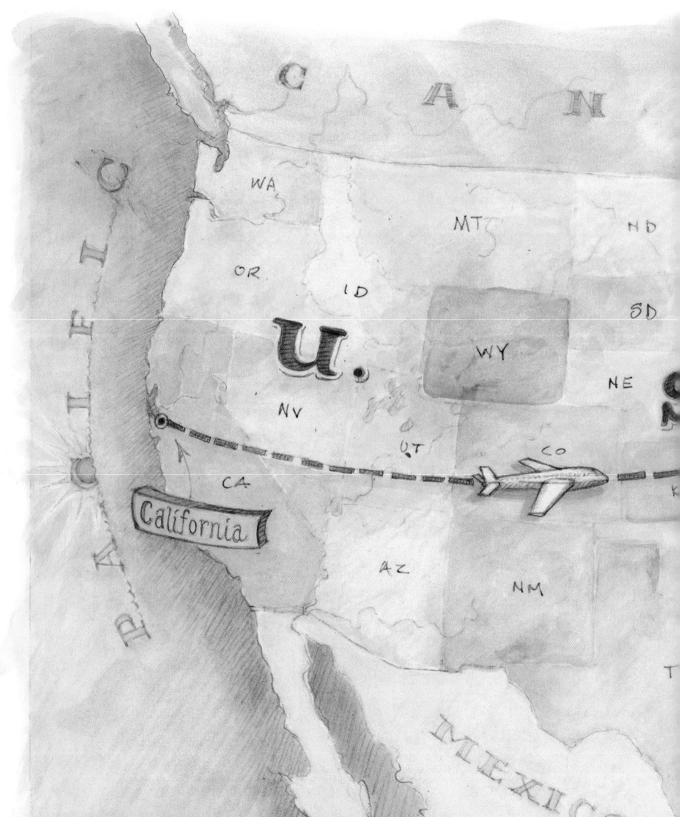

The airport was busy. The family met the airline attendant, Kelly, who assured them that Jimmy and Julie would be safely "delivered" to their grandparents in Vermont.

"We love you! We'll miss you," Mom and Dad said as hugs and kisses were exchanged. They waved goodbye as Jimmy and Julie walked down the jetway. This was a very big day for everyone!

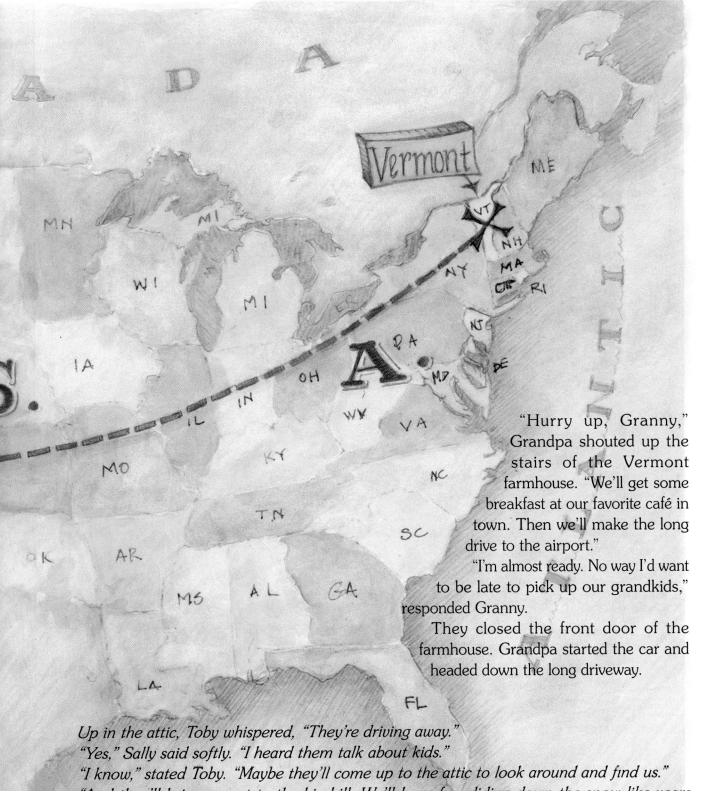

"Hurry up, Granny," Grandpa shouted up the stairs of the Vermont farmhouse. "We'll get some breakfast at our favorite café in town. Then we'll make the long drive to the airport."

"I'm almost ready. No way I'd want to be late to pick up our grandkids," responded Granny.

They closed the front door of the farmhouse. Grandpa started the car and headed down the long driveway.

Up in the attic, Toby whispered, "They're driving away."

"Yes," Sally said softly. "I heard them talk about kids."

"I know," stated Toby. "Maybe they'll come up to the attic to look around and find us."

"And they'll bring us out to the big hill. We'll have fun sliding down the snow like years ago," added an excited Sally.

"Right," agreed Toby. "They just have to find us up here. Maybe there's a way we can let them know we're here."

"We just have to think of a way," Toby and Sally exclaimed.

Chapter 3

Granny and Grandpa watched as the big airplane landed. Fifteen minutes later, they saw two excited children and their airline attendant come through the gate. Granny and Grandpa exchanged big hugs and kisses with Jimmy and Julie.

"Thank you, Kelly, for helping us on the flight," exclaimed the kids and waved as Kelly headed back to the jetway.

"Yes, thanks so much, Kelly," said Granny and Grandpa.

"Come on, Jimmy and Julie," said Granny. "We need to get your luggage."

"Hurry along," said Grandpa. "It's a four-hour car ride through Vermont to the family farmhouse. We'll stop for dinner along the way."

After dinner, while riding back, Jimmy and Julie asked all sorts of questions about the family home: "How old is it? How big is it? How many people have lived there? Is it far away from town and other kids? Are there toys to play with?"

Granny and Grandpa answered their questions the best they could. "The farmhouse where I grew up is still like it was many years ago," Granny stated. "I hope you'll have as much fun having an old-fashioned Christmas like I experienced when I was your age. You'll just have to see what we have planned."

"Wow, a trip to the olden days," Jimmy and Julie exclaimed with a hint of uncertainty.

A light snow started to fall as they continued their drive through the Vermont countryside.

Finally, Grandpa turned into the long driveway. He said quietly to Granny, "We're here. How are the kids?"

"Both asleep. We'll help them get inside and ready for bed. They've had a really busy day." Tomorrow is going to be an even busier day, thought Granny.

In the attic, Toby and Sally listened as four very tired people entered the old farmhouse and prepared for bed.

"They're back and with their grandkids! Oh, I sure want to go outside and have them ride us down that big snowy hill," said Sally.

"There's got to be a way we can get them to find us," Toby responded.

Chapter 4

"Time to get up, Jimmy and Julie," Granny called up the stairs. "I've got pancakes, bacon, and real Vermont maple syrup all ready. You'll need a hearty breakfast to do what we've planned today!"

A still-sleepy Jimmy and Julie woke up in their bedroom and looked around. "This sure is different from home," said Jimmy.

"Yeah, it is. I don't see any toys," Julie said.

"Neither do I. And I don't see a TV either," Jimmy stated. "But I'm hungry. Let's go down to breakfast."

They clamored downstairs in their pj's and robes. They saw Granny flipping pancakes as Grandpa placed pieces of wood into the cookstove. "That's a really different-looking stove," Jimmy said.

"Why does it need wood?" asked Julie.

Granny answered, "This is an old-fashioned stove. It's the same one my mom cooked on when I was growing up."

Grandpa continued, "Yup. One side of this stove heats up with wood, and the other side uses gas from the propane tank out in the back. In fact, half the lights in the farmhouse are old-style gaslights. They give off a nice glow and help to keep the place warm."

"You mean there's no electricity here?" asked Jimmy.

"Well, your great-grandma didn't want to give up the stove she used every day, so the stove and some of the lights stayed when the old farmhouse was converted to electricity," Grandpa explained.

Thinking back to what Jimmy hadn't seen in the bedroom, he asked cautiously, "What about a TV? You do have a TV, right?"

"We had a small TV," replied Grandma. "But when your great-grandparents gave me this place, Grandpa and I decided we didn't need it since we stay here only a few weeks of the year."

"What are we gonna do without a TV? Does that mean no DVD, too?" asked Julie.

"But, you do have an internet connection, don't you?" inquired Jimmy nervously.

"No, we don't have internet. But there's so much to do here, you won't miss them. We've planned an unplugged, old-fashioned Christmas, so the rule is no iPads. Come—let's eat breakfast. Don't worry, we have lots planned for you. Make sure you dress warmly," said Grandpa.

They finished their breakfast and then headed upstairs and got dressed to go outside.

"But what are we gonna do without a TV or DVD?" Jimmy asked Julie.

"And we can't even use our iPads," added an upset Julie.

"Well, we'll see about that," Jimmy said defiantly.

Toby had been thinking about how to get the children to find them in the attic. "Sally, I have an idea," an excited Toby said. "What if I made sounds like a TV turning on? Like scratchy static? Or yelled, 'This is your local news at five o'clock'?"

Sally laughed. "Toby, they can't hear us. Don't you remember the time that Billy and his friends were racing downhill on top of you? They were heading right for the big maple tree at the bottom, and you kept screaming, 'Look out! Look out! You're gonna smash me into splinters!' But they didn't hear you. It was Billy's father who saved the day. He ran and pushed you away from the tree at the last moment."

"Oh, yes, I remember now. I was so scared, and the louder I screamed, the more they pushed with their hands and sped down the hill! It's been so long I forgot only we can hear each other."

"Yes, and that means we have to find another way to get their attention."

Chapter 5

"So what is it you have planned for us today?" asked Jimmy as he came downstairs.

Grandpa pointed out the kitchen window to the woods behind the house. "We're going to hike out to the woods and find ourselves a Christmas tree. I'll cut down the one you want. Then we'll all drag it back to the house and set it up."

"We've never cut our own tree before," said Jimmy. "That sounds fun!"

"Where are the decorations, Granny?" Julie asked.

"We're going to make our own decorations. But first, let's get the exact tree you two want."

It was a brisk, sunny winter day as they tromped out to the woods. "How about this one?" Julie asked.

"Or this one. I want this one," Jimmy exclaimed.

They looked at a dozen or so trees, discussing the different types and sizes that would work best in the living room. Finally, Jimmy and Julie found the right tree.

Grandpa agreed. "This is a perfectly shaped tree."

"It will look beautiful," said Granny.

Grandpa took the axe and cut down the tree. He tied some rope around the trunk. They all huffed and puffed as they dragged it through the snow back to the front door.

Jimmy helped Grandpa set up the tree in the large living room. One side of the room had a long dining table. Right in the center of the wall was a beautiful stone fireplace with a rough-hewn timber mantle. On the other side of the room was a big window facing the front yard. On either side of the window were shelves filled with books, knickknacks, and framed photos of relatives and friends. Old wood rockers, comfortable chairs, and a large sofa facing the fireplace completed the room.

In the kitchen, Julie helped Granny make popcorn and a stiff dough of water, salt, and flour. "What's the dough for, Granny? It's too salty to eat."

"That's what we're going to use to make our decorations. We can shape them into anything you want. We have to be sure to put a hole in each one so we can hang it on the tree. Then we bake them in the oven to harden. Afterwards, we can paint and put sparkles or sequins on them. I brought all the things we needed."

"And we can eat the popcorn, right?"

"We can eat some of it, but the rest we're going to string together with fresh cranberries to make a garland for the tree."

When the tree was set up, Grandpa and Jimmy joined in stringing the garland and making all sorts of tree decorations—stars, bells, wreaths, candy canes, angels, reindeer, even dinosaurs and Ninja Turtles! While the decorations baked in the wood-burning oven, Jimmy and Julie helped place the garland on the tree. Granny put up the old bubble lights she had saved from a long time ago, while Grandpa started a roaring fire in the fireplace.

The dough decorations were now ready to paint. Jimmy and Julie did just that and glued their choice of sparkles and sequins on each. Then they threaded red and green ribbon through the holes to hang them on the branches of the tree.

"When we fly back home, can we take these with us? I want to use them on our tree there," Julie said.

"Absolutely," answered Granny. "But the popcorn and cranberry garland won't make it back."

"What will we do with the garland?" Julie asked Grandpa.

"After we've enjoyed them on the tree, we'll leave them outside to share with the birds and squirrels." Jimmy and Julie giggled at the thought of the animals enjoying some of their homemade decorations.

"Okay, children, you finish decorating the tree and watch the fire with Grandpa. I'll finish making my famous Christmas turkey stew."

From the attic, Toby and Sally listened to the fun. "I sure hope they made decorations in the shape of a toboggan," said Toby.

"I don't think so. We are the old style of winter toys. That's why we've been stored for so many years in this attic. But maybe ..." Sally's voice trailed off.

"We have to find a way to let them know we are here. We just have to," they both stated forcefully.

An hour later, Granny called out, "Dinner's ready," and headed into the living room. She placed the bowl of stew on the dining table that she had set with candles and festive plates, glasses, and silverware.

Julie and Jimmy ran over to the table, hungry and ready to eat. "Wait a minute," said Grandpa. "Now that the tree is all decorated, I'm going to turn off the lamps and plug in the old bubble lights."

"Yes, and I'm going to light all the candles," Granny said.

The four of them sat down to a wonderful meal. The glow of bubble lights, candles, and a crackling fire created a cozy, warm atmosphere.

"What's for dessert?" asked Julie

"I've made special holiday cookies. Plus, I have marshmallows. So it's time to roast them over the fire," said Granny. "And we'll have hot chocolate, too."

"But what are we going to do with no TV?" a worried Jimmy asked.

Grandpa told everyone, "There's an old radio over in the corner that still works. We can listen to the Christmas music on the local station. We can sing Christmas carols."

Granny chimed in, "And we can all tell stories! We'll describe what Christmas was like when we were your ages."

And that's what happened. The kids roasted marshmallows and ate homemade cookies. They sang "Jingle Bells," "Deck the Halls," and "We Wish You a Merry Christmas" in loud voices. Granny and Grandpa shared stories about marching in the village Christmas parade and making ice castles and snowmen for the town's winter festival. Soon, Jimmy and Julie nodded off to sleep. Granny and Grandpa helped them to their bedroom and into their pj's. It had been a long and busy day for all. Granny wondered, though, what would they do tomorrow with no TV.

As the family settled in for the night downstairs, Toby had an idea. "Sally, I have thought of a way to get the family's attention. It will take the two of us working together. But it just might work if we can time it right!"

"We'll make it work," replied Sally. And they discussed the details of their plan late into the night.

Chapter 6

Jimmy got up early the next morning. It was very quiet in the house. He looked for his iPad and after finding it, he turned it on and waited for it to power up. He had some old games saved and a movie he could watch.

Julie woke up, and when she saw Jimmy on his iPad, she exclaimed loudly, "You're not supposed to be on your iPad. Granny and Grandpa will be angry if they find out."

"What am I supposed to do? No internet, no TV, no DVD, just an old, scratchy-sounding radio. I bet there's not even a telephone here. I can't believe it," he shrieked.

The commotion woke up Granny and Grandpa. They ran into Jimmy and Julie's bedroom, asking, "What's wrong? What's the matter?"

Jimmy bellowed, "There's no internet, no TV, no DVD! And we can't even use our iPads. I bet you don't have a phone here. We're all alone and cut off from the rest of the world!"

"That's not true," said Granny. "We have cell phones. They work when we go into town."

"What are we supposed to do now? We're bored and stuck in this old farmhouse with nothing to do," Jimmy complained. Julie nodded in agreement.

Suddenly, a very loud crash sounded from above them.

Chapter 7

"That sound came from the attic," Grandpa said. "We better go see what caused the noise."

"Is this place haunted?" Jimmy asked nervously.

"Are there monsters up there?" asked a very scared Julie.

Granny assured them there were no monsters or ghosts. "We'll just have to go up to the attic and investigate. I'll pull down the attic steps."

"I'll get that powerful flashlight," said a confident Grandpa. He returned with one of the biggest flashlights Jimmy had ever seen.

A gust of cold air and dust wafted out of the attic as Granny carefully pulled down the attic stairs, resting the bottom step on the hallway floor. Grandpa started up the stairs with Jimmy close behind him, and Julie following her brother. Granny stepped up after Julie and made sure both children held on to the thin stair rail.

Meanwhile, "Good job," exclaimed Toby to Sally.

"Yeah, that hurt a bit, but it was worth it. I hear them coming up the stairs," said a very happy Sally.

When Grandpa got to the top of the stairs, he turned on the flashlight and took a few steps into the attic. Jimmy, Julie, and Granny inched their way up the stairs and carefully stepped into the attic. They watched as Grandpa shone the light around the attic. And there in front of the large stone chimney Granny spotted the cause the crash.

"Oh my gosh!" she exclaimed. "My winter playmates, Toby the toboggan and Sally the sled, must have fallen over from all the commotion downstairs! I had totally forgotten I stored them up here."

"What's a toboggan?" asked Jimmy.

"That doesn't look like any sled I've ever seen, Granny," said Julie.

Granny answered Jimmy and Julie's questions. She told them about the fun she had during the long winter months riding Toby and Sally with her friends and family.

Jimmy exclaimed, "I want to go outside and ride on Toby and Sally!"

"Me too," an excited Julie shouted. "Can we? Can we, please, pleeee-ase?"

"Yes, of course! Help me bring my old winter friends downstairs," said Granny. She no longer worried about what would keep Jimmy and Julie busy for the rest of their visit. The iPads and internet would have to wait until they returned home to California.

Chapter 8

Downstairs, Grandpa looked at the wear and tear on both Toby and Sally. He made a list of what he needed to ready these classic winter toys for riding. While the kids got dressed, Granny fixed a quick breakfast. Then they all piled into the car and rode to the small mountain village. Grandpa went to the hardware store. Granny took Jimmy and Julie to the clothing store, where they purchased snow boots, winter mittens, warm hats, and wool sweaters to wear under the jackets they brought from California.

Freed from the attic and in the corner of the living room, Toby and Sally had big grins that only toboggans and sleds could see. They both rejoiced. "It worked! We did it! Tomorrow is going to be the best day we've had in a very, very long time," said Toby.

When they returned to the farmhouse, Jimmy and Julie helped Grandpa fix Toby and Sally. They spent all afternoon and into the evening sanding, staining, waxing, polishing, and cleaning every part of Toby the toboggan and Sally the sled.

Granny busied herself in the kitchen preparing a big picnic lunch for tomorrow.

Finally, Grandpa said, "Toby and Sally are fixed and ready to be ridden! We'll leave them in the living room tonight."

"And bright and early tomorrow morning, we'll all climb up the big hill and spend the day playing and riding on Toby and Sally," Granny added. Tomorrow was going to be a very active—and fun—day!

After everyone had gone to bed, Sally and Toby took a good look at themselves. "Wow, I sure look good all polished. I can't wait for tomorrow morning," said an excited Sally the sled.

"Me too. I don't feel dusty and dried out anymore. Just look at my shiny leather seat," Toby the toboggan exclaimed.

Chapter 9

Jimmy and Julie awoke early and dressed in their new warm clothing. Granny and Grandpa greeted them in the kitchen where a big egg and bacon breakfast was already prepared. "You two will need a good breakfast to spend the day riding Toby and Sally. So eat up," said Granny.

Grandpa added, "You'll need lots of energy to walk up that hill, ride down, and then do it all again."

They quickly finished their breakfast. Jimmy and Julie put on their jackets and helped Grandpa carry Toby and Sally out the back door, while Granny filled the picnic basket.

Jimmy helped Grandpa pull Toby the toboggan up the hill. Julie and Granny did the same with Sally the sled, the picnic basket attached to her railings. They tromped up the big hill, leaving boot tracks in the freshly fallen snow.

At the top of the hill, Granny and Grandpa explained how to ride, steer, and stop Toby. Then it was time to take the first ride.

"Okay, Julie, you sit in the front of Toby, legs crossed," instructed Grandpa. "Now Jimmy, you sit behind her with your legs on either side of her."

"I'll sit behind Jimmy and then Grandpa in the back," said Granny.

"Are we all ready?" asked Grandpa. "Now push with your hands as I start Toby gliding downhill."

And off they went, laughing and giggling and yelling with joy as they bounced and flew down the hill.

As she watched Toby take off, Sally shouted, "Have fun, Toby! Go, go, go fast, you new-again toboggan!"

When they stopped at the bottom of the hill, Jimmy and Julie exclaimed, "Let's do it again!"

So they trudged up the hill again. But this time, Granny and Grandpa showed Jimmy and Julie how to sit on Sally the sled, how to turn her to the right and the left, and especially, how to slow down to a stop.

First, Julie and Grandpa rode Sally. Then Granny and Jimmy did the same.

"You look great, Sally," Toby yelled as she went flying down the hill with her special riders.

After a few hours, they stopped and ate the picnic lunch Granny had fixed— hot chocolate, warm soup, sandwiches, fruit, and cookies. As soon as they finished, up the hill they went again.

And so the day went. Riding down the hill on Toby and Sally in all configurations—Jimmy and Julie together or Granny and Grandpa together or all four at once. Sometimes they raced each other. Sometimes they fell off, rolling in the snow and laughing hysterically. Again and again and again.

When it started to get dark, Grandpa announced, "It's time for all of us to take Toby and Sally home and call it a day."

"No, I don't wanna stop. This is so much fun," complained Jimmy.

"Can we do it again tomorrow?" asked Julie.

"Yes, please, tomorrow! I want to ride on Toby and Sally again," Jimmy exclaimed.

"No, honey. Tomorrow morning we need to pack up your suitcases and drive back to the airport," said Granny.

"Already?" asked Jimmy.

"No, not yet! It's too soon," Julie said, disappointed.

But it was true. Their old-fashioned Christmas was coming to an end. So Jimmy, Julie, Granny, and Grandpa pulled Toby and Sally back to the farmhouse. "Would you like to have Toby and Sally inside the farmhouse for your last night here?" asked Granny.

"Yes," shouted Jimmy and Julie.

"How about we place Toby and Sally right in front of the stone fireplace?" Granny suggested. "You can sit on them and help us roast hot dogs over the fire."

So they all gathered around the fireplace, enjoyed their dinner, and reminisced about their day's experiences.

"May I take Sally home with me?" asked Julie.

Jimmy added, "Yes, please may I take Toby home to California?"

Granny sighed. "Honey, this is where Toby and Sally have lived all their lives. But anytime you want to visit, you can."

And with that, they settled down on Toby and Sally and watched the crackling fire, enjoying their last evening in the old farmhouse.

Toby and Sally couldn't have been happier about their day. And to be sitting in the living room with their family. "What a fantastic day. I'm a bit tired," Sally told Toby.

"I'm exhausted, too, but a hundred times as happy," responded Toby.

Chapter 10

"Wake up," said Granny early the next morning.

"Time to ready your backpacks to fly back to your mom and dad," said Grandpa. "Don't forget your iPads!"

"Huh, iPads? Oh, right, our iPads," responded a groggy Jimmy as he and Julie slowly got out of bed and dressed for the return home. They walked down stairs and sat down for their last breakfast in the old farmhouse kitchen.

"I'm sad," said Julie.

"You are?" asked Granny. "Didn't you have fun while you were here?"

"I had the best time," said Julie.

"Me too," said Jimmy. "But it went so fast!"

"Good times always go fast," said Grandpa.

"When I grow up and have kids, can they come and play in the snow with Toby and Sally, like Jimmy and I did?" asked Julie.

"You sure can," said Grandpa. "Because someday, when you're all grown up, we plan to give Jimmy and you this old farmhouse. And, of course, Toby and Sally are part of this home."

"Yippee!" yelled both kids

Then all put on their coats and headed out the front door, ready for the ride back to the airport. Granny and Grandpa packed the luggage in the trunk of the car as Jimmy and Julie got in the backseat.

As they drove away, Granny said, "Look behind you. I think someone wants to say goodbye."

As they looked back at the old farmhouse, they saw Toby the toboggan and Sally the sled leaning up against the fence where Grandpa had placed them early that morning. It almost seemed like they were smiling.

Jimmy and Julie waved goodbye until the car turned out of the long driveway. They turned to Granny and Grandpa and exclaimed, "This was this best old-fashioned Christmas ever!"

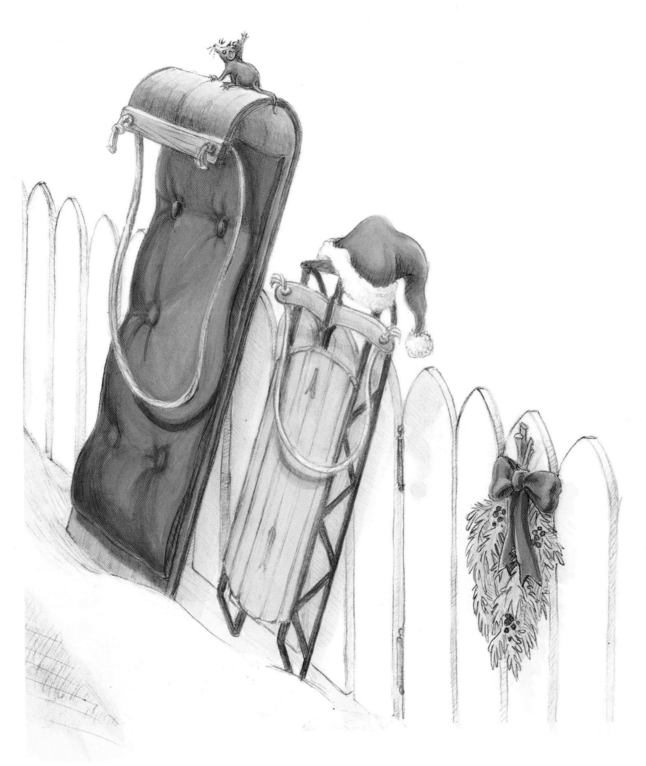

"We did it," said a very happy Sally to Toby as they watched the car drive away.
Grinning from slat to slat, Toby responded, "Yes, and we will never be forgotten again!"

About the Author

Karen Votraw-Gysen has 40 years experience in education as an English teacher, Nationally Board Certified counselor and program administrator. During her career she served on numerous professional & non-profit organizations. She has presented at State, Regional and National Conventions. She has been published in a variety of local and regional magazines. Her article in **Adirondack Life** magazine was also published in the magazine's first 10 year anthology <u>Adirondack Places and Pleasures</u>. She has volunteered in local fundraising events and children's programs. Additionally, she loves to travel with her husband, and is an avid camper and canoeist working at one time for CANOE, USA and Voyageur Outward Bound. In 2007, she was appointed by the Governor of Nevada to serve as a member of the Commission on Professional Standards in Education. Her goal in retirement is to amuse herself and children through writing.

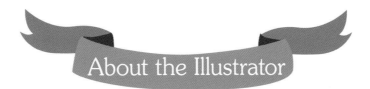

About the Illustrator

Christine Bond Sullivan received her training at Art Center College of Design in Pasadena, California. She and her husband currently reside in the foothills of the beautiful Sierra Nevada Mountain Range. She loves young people, flowers, landscapes, and Lake Tahoe. She is the mother of five grown children, each of whom she home-schooled for a portion of their education. Christine has illustrated two other children's books, Dr. Dreamer, which introduces children to the medical role of the anesthesiologist, part of the Which Doctor series; and A Haircut for Henry, about a young boy's first trip to the barber. She has created commissioned work in water color and acrylics, for individuals as well as for organizations. She has taught art classes for children and for adults, painted murals, and created sets for a local children's theater, for her church, and for a local Senior Center